The New Dog

a story about friendship

by Alex Stephenson

This is Sandy.
She is a dog.

Sandy really likes
being a dog.

She likes playing
dog games.

She likes dog food.

She even likes the
two big dogs who
take care of her.

One day, there was
a NEW dog in her home.

Sandy wasn't sure
about the new dog...

...but she thought: "If I could just **MAKE** her like me, we could be best friends."

So, she tried to show the
new dog the best place
to get a drink of water.

She tried to teach the new dog
all the best tricks to get treats.

She even tried to show the
new dog her favorite
bury spots.

For some reason though,
the new dog didn't seem
to care.

Out of ideas, Sandy was starting
to fear that she'd never
get the new dog to like her.

But then one day,
Sandy had an idea!

She would watch the new dog
to find out what kind of things
SHE liked to do.

But that

got really boring,

really quickly.

Feeling defeated, Sandy
decided she should just
give up.

She said "How come you don't
want to be friends?
I was excited to meet a new dog."

The new dog said
"But, I'm NOT a dog..."

"My name's Jade, and I'm a cat. I had no idea you wanted to be friends!"

"But, I tried to get you to do the things I do - and made myself do the things you do..."

"Did you ever just ask if I wanted to be your friend?" Jade said.

"I..."
Sandy said.

"I... I..."
She tried again.

"But, we don't like any of the same stuff." said Sandy.

"Friends don't have to like all the same stuff," said Jade.

"they just have to like
each other."

After that, Sandy and Jade
decided to learn all about
each other.

They told each other about
the things they liked...

...and the things they didn't.

And because they didn't
force it,

or try to change each other,

they got to know what
best friends really were.

The end.

for Sandy and Jade

6763198R00025

Printed in Germany
by Amazon Distribution
GmbH, Leipzig